GEORGE CRUM
and the
Saratoga Chip

by Gaylia Taylor illustrated by Frank Morrison

Lee & Low Books Inc.

New York

Author's Sources

Books

Bradley, Hugh. *Such Was Saratoga*. New York: Doubleday, Doran and Company, 1940.

Britten, Evelyn Barrett. *Chronicles of Saratoga*. Saratoga Springs: Published privately by Evelyn Barrett Britten, 1959. Originally published as a series of articles in *The Saratogian* beginning in 1947.

Sylvester, Nathaniel Bartlett. *History of Saratoga County with Historical Notes On Its Various Towns Together with Biographical Sketches of Its Prominent Men and Leading Citizens Prepared by Samuel T. Wiley and W. Scott Garner*. Richmond, Indiana: Gresham Publishing Company, 1893.

Newspaper Articles

Roy, Yancey. "The Chip Behind the Myth: Historian Clarifies Discovery Shrouded in Grease," *The Times Union*, January 30, 1992.

Marsh, Sondrah. "Potato Chip Was Born Out of Crisp Revenge!" *The St. Petersburg Times*, August, 1978.

Web Sites

Brookside Museum: Home of the Saratoga Springs Historical Society Web Site, "Photo of the Month September 2002." Featuring photo of George Crum outside of his restaurant and text from a presentation given by David Mitchell, Executive Director of Brookside Museum, 1992. http://www.brooksidemuseum.org/photo/2002/september 2002.html

Text copyright © 2006 by Gaylia Taylor
Illustrations copyright © 2006 by Frank Morrison

Manufactured in China by RR Donnelley Limited, May 2017

Book design by David Neuhaus/NeuStudio
Book production by The Kids at Our House

The text is set in Cochin
The illustrations are rendered in acrylic

HC 10 9 8 7 6 5 4
PB 10 9 8 7 6 5
First Edition

Library of Congress Cataloging-in-Publication Data
Taylor, Gaylia.
    George Crum and the Saratoga chip / by Gaylia Taylor ; illustrated by Frank Morrison.— 1st ed.
        p. cm.
    ISBN 978-1-58430-255-1 (HC) ISBN 978-1-60060-656-4 (PB)
    1. Crum, George, chef—Juvenile literature. 2. Cooks—New York (State)—Saratoga Springs—Biography—Juvenile literature. 3. Potato chips—History—Juvenile literature.
    I. Morrison, Frank, 1971- ill. II. Title.
    TX140.C78T39 2006
    641.5'092—dc22   2005015313

For my husband, Robert—G.T.

To my favorite chip lovers Nia, Nyree, Tyreek, and Nas—F.M.

George stood before the students in the one-room schoolhouse. His palms were sweaty and his knees were weak. All the first graders could count to one hundred, except George.

His sister, Kate, sat across the room with the older students. Kate helped George practice his numbers at home every night and was always encouraging him. He looked at Kate, took a deep breath, and started to count.

George counted up to sixty-eight, then got confused and couldn't remember which number came next. The other children laughed, and George felt his skin begin to prickle.

It was difficult for George and Kate growing up in the 1830s. They were part Native American and part African American, at a time when people of color in the United States were often treated as inferior to white people. George had a feisty streak, and he would get frustrated when the other children laughed at him or acted as if they were better than he was. He wanted them to know he was just as good as they were.

When George was with Kate, his feistiness turned playful and mischievous. He joked with his sister. He teased her. He taught Kate to climb a tree and shoot a bow and arrow better than any boy in the county.

George loved the outdoors. He spent hours fishing and exploring the nearby Adirondack mountains. He watched the wild turkeys strut around with their hens, fascinated by their iridescent colors. He listened carefully and practiced imitating their calls. This amused George for hours.

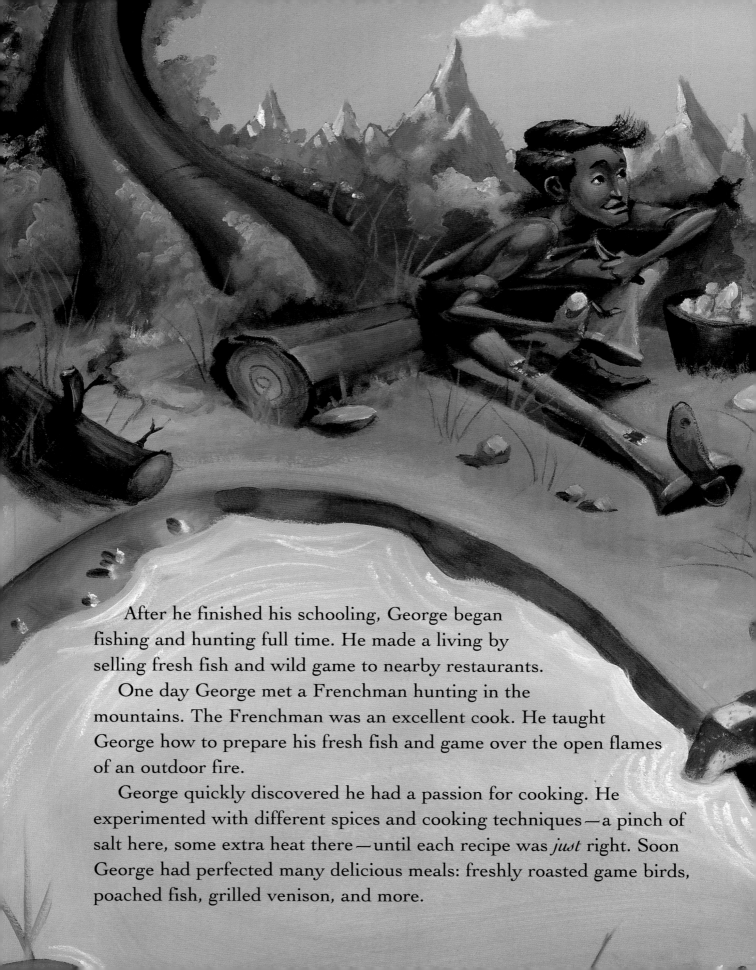

After he finished his schooling, George began
fishing and hunting full time. He made a living by
selling fresh fish and wild game to nearby restaurants.

One day George met a Frenchman hunting in the
mountains. The Frenchman was an excellent cook. He taught
George how to prepare his fresh fish and game over the open flames
of an outdoor fire.

George quickly discovered he had a passion for cooking. He
experimented with different spices and cooking techniques—a pinch of
salt here, some extra heat there—until each recipe was *just* right. Soon
George had perfected many delicious meals: freshly roasted game birds,
poached fish, grilled venison, and more.

George wanted to show all of Saratoga Springs what a good cook he was. He decided the best way to do this was to become a chef in a restaurant. It wasn't easy for George to get a job as a chef in those days. Most restaurant owners wouldn't hire a man of color to be anything but a waiter. George didn't let that stop him.

Sure enough, George's excellent cooking skills shone through. He landed a job at Moon's Lake House, one of the best restaurants in Saratoga Springs. George's heart swelled when he thought about all the people who would now enjoy his meals.

George quickly became famous for his wild game and fish dishes. Prominent people, including Cornelius Vanderbilt, one of the richest men in America, traveled great distances to eat at Moon's Lake House. George's most sought after dish was his canvasback duck. It was so tender and juicy, that no other chef in the area could match its taste.

George enjoyed creating new recipes at Moon's Lake House, but he soon realized he had little patience for the fussy customers. They demanded immediate attention to their needs and were quick to complain. They acted as if they were better than the people serving them—something George did not like in the least. Luckily Kate worked as a waitress at the restaurant. She tried her best to keep George in good spirits and his feistiness from getting the better of him.

One evening a
customer complained to
Kate that his meal was not hot
enough. Kate apologized, picked up
the man's plate, and headed swiftly
toward the kitchen.

George knew the meal he had sent out had been
perfectly prepared, but he also knew he had to please the
restaurant's customers. So he carefully scraped the tender
quail and vegetables into a black iron skillet over hot flames.

After a few minutes George tested the temperature of the food and
decided it was just right. With great care he scooped everything onto a
fresh plate and placed it on a silver platter. George wiped the sweat from
his brow, straightened his starched white chef's apron, and stepped out
into the dining room.

Proud of his efforts, George placed the hot meal in front of the customer. The man took a small bite, then announced that the food was still not hot enough. George's skin prickled. He tried to hide his annoyance and gave the man a weak smile. Without a word George took the plate and quickly turned. All of a sudden he lost his balance and tripped.

A ripple of laughter passed through the dining room when George hit the floor. His cheeks grew hot and flushed. As George brushed himself off, he heard a woman whisper loudly about the poor quality of the staff. George felt just like he was back in first grade, trying to count to one hundred. He headed to the safety of the kitchen, hoping the night would soon be over.

George continued to have good days and bad days with the customers at Moon's Lake House. He still loved cooking, but his patience for pleasing difficult customers was growing thin. Then one hot summer day in August 1853, something happened that changed George's life forever.

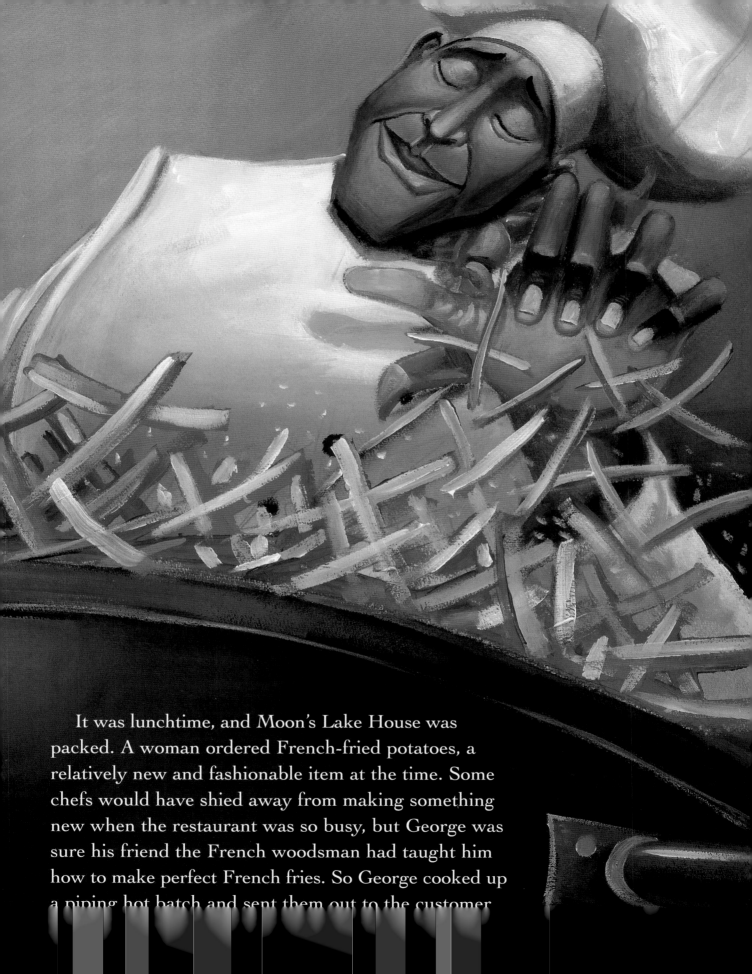

It was lunchtime, and Moon's Lake House was
packed. A woman ordered French-fried potatoes, a
relatively new and fashionable item at the time. Some
chefs would have shied away from making something
new when the restaurant was so busy, but George was
sure his friend the French woodsman had taught him
how to make perfect French fries. So George cooked up
a piping hot batch and sent them out to the customer.

The woman looked at the plate of French fries and before even taking a bite complained to the waiter that the potatoes were cut too thick. The waiter knew not to argue with a customer, so he graciously took the French fries back to the kitchen.

George was shocked to see the potatoes returned. He had just about had enough of fussy customers. George grabbed a potato and started slicing. Kate saw a spark of feistiness in her brother's eyes that she hadn't seen in quite a while.

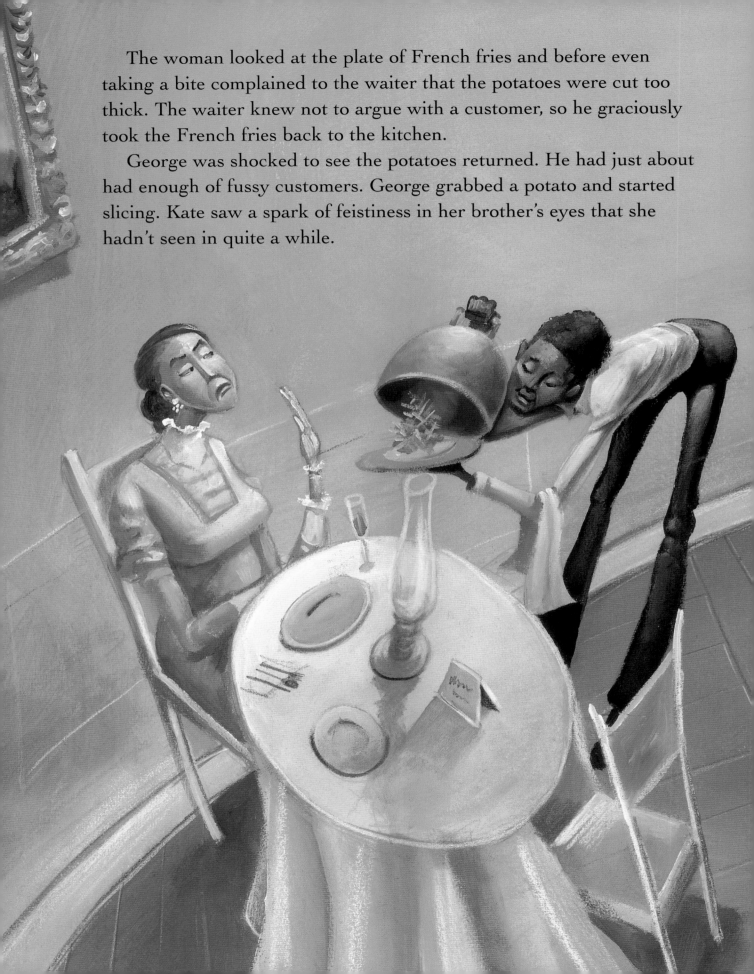

George was very, *very* careful to cut the potatoes very, *very* thin. They were so thin that when he held a slice up to the light, he could see straight through it. Then he put the slices into a pot full of hot oil. He purposely cooked the potatoes longer and at a higher temperature than was needed for perfect French fries.

When the potatoes were crisp and brown, George removed them from the oil and piled them onto a plate. He decided to serve his special new creation to the customer himself.

Kate and other members of the staff peered anxiously through the kitchen doors. Their eyes were glued to the woman. No one wanted to miss her reaction.

George presented the plate of fried potatoes and waited for the woman's complaints.

She took a small bite. Then another. And another. Finally she declared them the most delicious potato delicacy she had ever tasted!

George was so stunned he didn't know what to say. He mumbled his thanks and returned to the kitchen in a daze.

From that day on everybody who came to Moon's Lake House wanted the new potato creation. Soon people were calling them Saratoga chips, in honor of Saratoga Springs where the restaurant was located.

George continued cooking at Moon's Lake House for several years, but then he got to thinking it was time to leave. He still didn't like cooking for people who looked down on other folks and treated them badly.

George started dreaming of his own restaurant—a comfortable place where anyone could enjoy a good meal and everyone would be treated equally. George was confident that with his cooking skills and the popularity of his Saratoga chips, he could make his own way in the restaurant business.

After leaving Moon's Lake House, George bought some land and built a restaurant that he named Crum's Place. On the surrounding farmland he raised chickens, cows, and pigs, and grew vegetables and fruit. All the food served in the restaurant came fresh from the farm, including the potatoes for George's famous chips.

George was proud of his restaurant. It was nestled among tall shade trees and had an inviting front porch facing a lake. It was a comfortable place where diners could enjoy good food, fun, and laughter.

There were always long lines at Crum's Place and customers had to wait their turns for seats in the dining room. So George devised a rule that made him very happy indeed: Rich or poor, light-skinned or dark, young or old, female or male, everybody had to wait just the same, because everyone was equal at Crum's Place!

And if any customers happened to fuss about waiting their turn, good old George would get a feisty look in his eyes and say, "If you can't wait, get your grub at Moon's!"

Author's Note

Although there is little definitive historical information about George Crum and the invention of the potato chip, I have created this story based on the more substantiated existing facts.

George was born to Abraham and Katherine Speck in 1828. His father was a jockey and used the last name Crum, which George later adopted. Some research notes that George was Native American while other research suggests he was also part African American. Searches of the census show that George and his sister, Kate, are listed as mulattoes, which supports the theory of their mixed Native American and African American ancestry.

Most research agrees that George Crum had a colorful personality and that he is credited with inventing Saratoga chips while trying to appease a patron who ordered French fries. Some versions of the story claim that Cornelius Vanderbilt himself was the disgruntled diner who complained about the French fries, though this is unlikely. Other accounts suggest that Kate may have played a larger role in the chips' invention.

At first Saratoga chips were a delicacy for the wealthy. George's recipe was printed in the *White House Cookbook* every year. But soon the chips became very popular, and in no time the tasty snack spread across the country. In 1895 William C. Tappenden of Cleveland, Ohio, became one of the first people to mass produce and distribute potato chips under the brand name Saratoga Chips. By the 1930s Herman Lay had begun his potato chip empire in Atlanta, Georgia.

George Crum eventually retired from the restaurant business and lived out his life on his farm. He loved the outdoors as much as ever and had one wish before he died. George said he had tasted every native wild animal in the area except skunk, and he wanted to try one. Granted his wish, George claimed that skunk was very tasty meat. George Crum died in 1914.

Gaylia Taylor